Karen's Sleepover

Also in the Babysitters Little Sister series:

Look out for:

Karen's Sleepover

Ann M. Martin

Illustrations by Susan Tang

Scholastic Children's Books,
Scholastic Publications Ltd,
7-9 Pratt Street, London NW1 0AE, UK

Scholastic Inc.,
555 Broadway, New York, NY10012-3999,
USA

Scholastic Canada Ltd,
123 Newkirk Road, Richmond Hill,
Ontario, Canada L4C 3G5

Ashton Scholastic Pty Ltd,
PO Box 579, Gosford, New South Wales,
Australia

Ashton Scholastic Ltd
Private Bag 94407, Greenmount, Auckland,
New Zealand

First published in the USA by Scholastic Inc, 1990
First published in the UK by Scholastic Publications Ltd, 1992

Text copyright © Ann M. Martin 1990

BABYSITTERS LITTLE SISTER is a trademark of Scholastic Inc.

ISBN 0 590 55132 9

Printed by Cox & Wyman Ltd, Reading, Berks
Typeset by A.J. Latham Ltd, Dunstable, Beds

10 9 8 7 6 5 4

*This book
is in honour of the birth of
Emma Feiwel*

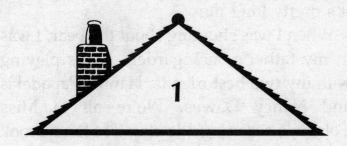

Party Time

"Help! Help me! I'm lost! And a bear is after me!"

That wasn't true, of course. I wasn't lost, and no bear was after me. There aren't any bears in Stoneybrook, Connecticut. At least, I don't think there are any bears.

Hi. My name is Karen Brewer. I'm seven years old, which is a very good age. I have a little brother called Andrew, an adopted sister, a stepsister, and three stepbrothers. I wear glasses and I have some freckles. Once I had a horrible haircut, but now my

1

hair has grown out and is back to normal. It's pretty long now.

When I was shouting about the bear, I was in my father's back garden. I was playing with my two best friends, Hannie Papadakis and Nancy Dawes. We're all in Miss Colman's second-grade class at Stoneybrook Academy. It was a Saturday afternoon and we were pretending we were camping. Nancy had said, "Let's play 'Going Camping'." So we made a tent by draping a blanket over two chairs. Then Elizabeth, my stepmother, let us take some pots and pans out of the kitchen and put them in our tent. Now we were running around pretending we were in the woods.

"I'll save you!" Hannie yelled to me. "Hey, bear!" she cried. "Go away! Shoo!"

"You can't say 'shoo' to a bear!" exclaimed Nancy. "You say 'shoo' to a fly. Or maybe to a cat or even a small dog. But not to a *bear*."

"What do you say to a bear?" Hannie wondered.

Nancy didn't know.

"Well, I'm tired," I said. "I think it's bedtime."

My friends and I made beds out of piles of leaves. Then we lay down in the leaves. They got stuck in our hair and on our sweaters.

"I wish we had real sleeping bags out here," said Hannie.

"That would be brilliant," I agreed.

"I've got a real sleeping bag, but it's at my house," said Nancy. (Nancy doesn't live nearby. She lives next door to Mummy's house.)

"We've got real sleeping bags, too," I said, "but they're in our attic. The last time we used them was when Kristy had a sleepover." (Kristy is my big stepsister.)

"Sleepovers sound like fun," said Hannie. "I've never, ever been to one."

"Me, neither," said Nancy and I at the same time.

"I bet you get to do all sorts of great things at a sleepover," said Hannie.

"The sleeping-bag part would be fun," I added.

"Yeah," said Nancy.

"Do you think we're too young to go to a sleepover?" asked Hannie.

"Of course not!" I said. Seven is old enough to do anything!"

"You can't drive when you're seven," said Nancy.

"Noooo. But you could have a sleepover. . . . And I'm going to have one!" I said suddenly.

"You *are*?" cried Hannie and Nancy.

"Yes. Yes, I am. I will have one right here at Daddy's house — if Daddy and Elizabeth say I can."

"Wow!" said Hannie.

Later that day, Hannie walked home, and Mrs Dawes picked Nancy up. When my friends were gone, I found Daddy and Elizabeth. They were in the kitchen.

"Um, I have something to ask you," I said to them.

"What is it?" asked Daddy.

"Can I have a sleepover party for my friends? And can I have it here?"

Daddy and Elizabeth looked at each other. They were talking with their eyes. At last Daddy said, "I don't see why not."

"All *right*!" I shouted.

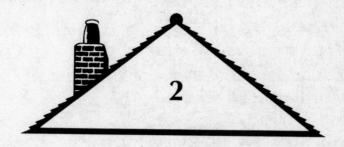

The Two-Twos

Late on Sunday afternoon, Mummy came to pick up me and Andrew, and take us to her house.

Toot, toot! went her car horn in the drive.

"Mummy's here," I said.

" 'Bye! Goodbye!" Andrew and I called. There was a lot of hugging and kissing when we left Daddy's house. "See you in two weeks!" I called.

The reason Mummy and Daddy live in different houses is because they're divorced.

First they were married, and then they had
Andrew and me, then they decided to get
divorced. They wanted to live in separate
houses.

Guess what? After a while, they both got
married again. Daddy married Elizabeth.
She already had four children of her own.
They are Sam and Charlie, who go to high
school; David Michael, who's seven like me;
and Kristy, who's thirteen. Kristy is one of
my most favourite people. She likes

babysitting and she's even the chairman of a business called The Babysitters Club. I like it best when Kristy babysits for *me*! Sam, Charlie, David Michael, and Kristy are my stepbrothers and stepsister.

Andrew and I have also got an adopted sister. Her name is Emily Michelle and she's two years old. She came all the way from a country called Vietnam. Daddy and Elizabeth wanted Emily very much. I'm still deciding if I like her. She's my little sister and Kristy is my big sister. I'm the middle sister.

It's a good thing that Daddy's got lots and lots of money, because his family is *so* big. There's Nannie, too. She's Elizabeth's mother and she helps look after us. And there's Boo-Boo, Daddy's fat, mean old cat, and Shannon, David Michael's puppy.

At Mummy's house there's just Mummy and Seth (he's our stepfather), Rocky and Midgie, Seth's cat and dog, and Emily Junior, my rat, who's named after Emily Michelle. Oh, and there are Andrew and me, of course. We live with Mummy and Seth most of the time. We only live at Daddy's every other weekend and for two weeks during the summer.

Daddy's house is big. Mummy's is little.

Since Andrew and I live at two houses, I call us the two-twos. I got the name from a book Miss Colman read to our class once. It was called *Jacob Two-Two Meets the Hooded Fang*. I thought "two-two" was the perfect name for Andrew and me. We are Andrew Two-Two and Karen Two-Two because we've got two of almost everything. We have two houses. We have two families. We have two dogs, one at the little house and one at the big house. We have two cats, one at each house. I have a best friend at each house. We have clothes and toys and books and bicycles at each house. This makes going back and forth much easier. We hardly ever have to pack anything. I even have two stuffed cats, Moosie and Goosie. Moosie stays in my room at the big house. Goosie stays in my room at the little house.

Being a two-two isn't always easy, though.

For instance, I only had one special blanket — Tickly. I kept leaving Tickly at one house or the other. Finally I had to rip Tickly in half so I could have a piece at each house. And there is only one Emily Junior. I miss her a lot when I'm at the big house, even though I know Mummy and Seth take good care of her.

Here's one nice thing about being a two-two. I like the little house for peace and quiet, and I *love* the big house for excitement. I'm lucky to have both. I wish Mummy and Daddy were still married, but being a two-two isn't all that bad.

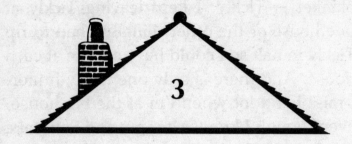

Little House, Big House

"Guess what!? Guess what!?" I cried as soon as I ran into Miss Colman's class on Monday morning.

"Indoor voice. Use your indoor voice, Karen," Miss Colman reminded me. She was sitting at her desk. A lot of children were in our room, but school hadn't started yet.

"Okay," I said to Miss Colman. "Sorry." I like Miss Colman a lot. She's nice to me. I'm the youngest in my class (I skipped most of kindergarten), and I have to wear *two* pairs of glasses — one for reading and one for the rest of the time. Miss Colman helps me to remember things, like which pair of glasses to wear and when to use my indoor voice.

She never shouts.

"Hannie! Nancy!" I said in a loud whisper.

"What?" they answered.

"Daddy said I could have a sleepover party!"

I'd known that since Saturday, but I'd kept it a secret. I thought it might be a nice surprise for Monday morning. And it was.

"You're kidding!" exclaimed Nancy.

"Really?" cried Hannie.

We were all whispering excitedly.

"What's the secret?" asked Natalie Springer. She walked over to us.

I looked at Hannie and Nancy. Should I tell Natalie? After all, I hadn't decided who to invite to my sleepover yet — except for my two best friends.

Hannie and Nancy shrugged. So I said

grandly, "I'm having a sleepover party. . . and *you're* invited!" Daddy and Elizabeth had said I could invite ten people to my sleepover.

"Thanks!" said Natalie.

Then I heard a voice behind me. It was a high-pitched boy's voice. "I'm having a sleepover party. . . and *you're* invited!" I knew it was Ricky Torres and he was imitating me.

I also knew he was only teasing.

"Puh-*lease* can I come to your sleepover?" teased Ricky. "I'll bring my best nightdress and —"

"Sleepovers are for girls," I informed him. "At least, mine is."

"For all girls?" asked Ricky.

"For all the girls in our class," I told him. I hadn't thought about it, but that seemed like a nice thing to do. I would invite all the girls in my class. There were nine of us. I liked the girls. And if I invited every one of them, then nobody would feel left out.

"I'm coming, too," said Ricky. "I'm going to gatecrash your party."

"No, you're not," I told him, even though I wouldn't have minded if he had. Ricky and I like each other.

"Then I'm going to come and spy on your party. I'm going to spy on you girls in your nightdresses.

"Eeee!" cried Nancy. "No!"

"What party?" asked Jannie Gilbert.

So I told her about the sleepover.

By the end of the day, everyone in

Miss Colman's class knew about my party — and I hadn't even sent out any invitations. Oh, well. Who cared? I would send invitations later anyway. For now, I was very happy. All the girls kept coming up to me and saying things like, "A *real* sleepover. Cool!" And, "Only my *big* sister ever goes to sleepovers. Now I can go, too!"

Nobody could wait for my sleepover party.

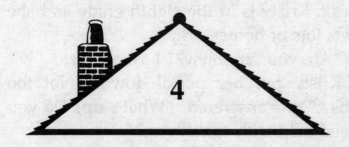

Party Plans

Eleven days later, Andrew and I were back at the big house for our weekend. On Friday night we played with David Michael and Emily. But on Saturday I had important things to do. I had to plan my sleepover party.

I decided to talk to Kristy. Kristy and her friends in the Babysitters Club have lots of sleepovers. Kristy would know what to do at a sleepover. She would also know what I needed to buy.

"Kristy?" I said.

Kristy was in her room, working at her desk. Kristy is in the eighth grade and she gets lots of homework.

"Are you *very* busy?" I asked her.

Kristy put her pencil down. "Not too busy," she answered. "What's up? Do you need help with something?"

I nodded. "My sleepover party. What do I need to buy?"

"Mostly food," Kristy replied. She ripped a piece of paper out of her notebook. "Let's make a list." (We sat down together on her bed.)

"What kind of food?" I asked.

"Pizzas," Kristy said immediately. "They'll be for dinner. Then for snacks, you will need popcorn, crisps, twiglets. . ." Kristy went on and on. We wrote everything down.

"Do we need any party decorations?" I asked.

Kristy shook her head. "Nope."

"We don't?" I must have looked very disappointed because Kristy let me add:

18

CREPE PAPER
and
BALLOONS

to the list. (The first time I spelt *crepe* like this: crape. Kristy helped me spell it properly.)

"Now," I said, "what do you *do* at a sleepover? I know you don't sleep."

"Well, you don't sleep much," Kristy replied, smiling. "You do lots of other things. You watch a spooky film and scare yourselves. You can make some fudge."

"Can we make Slice 'n' Bake cookies instead?" I interrupted.

"Whatever you like. Then you gossip. You raid the fridge. And you stay up as late as you can. My friends and I always play Truth or Dare and try on make-up," added Kristy, "but I think you're a bit too young for that."

"We are not!" I cried, but I didn't really care. "Boy," I said. "We'll have *loads* to do at the party. Thanks, Kristy."

19

I gave Daddy the list that Kristy and I had made. Then I went to my room and finished making the invitations for the party. They said:

Come to a sleepover! Bring your sleeping bag! (Let me know if you don't have one.) We will watch a film. We will eat pizza. We will make cookies. Maybe we will try on make-up.

Then I wrote down the place and time of the party so my friends would know where and when the sleepover would be held. When the invitations were finished, I put them in the postbox on our street. Then I came home.

"David Michael, Andrew," I said, when I found them playing in the living room. "You have to stay away from my party. No boys allowed."

Then I found Sam and told him the same thing. Sam told me I was a weirdo. I ignored him.

Then I found Charlie and told *him* the same thing, but I asked if he would tell us a ghost story and then leave the party as soon as he had finished.

"Okay," said Charlie.

Oh, boy! I thought. This is going to be the best sleepover ever!

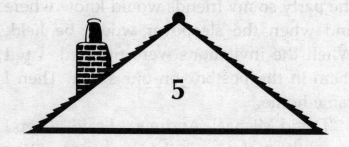

5

Nancy's Invitation

I had posted my invitations on Saturday. By Wednesday, every girl in Miss Colman's class had received one — except Nancy.

Nancy looked insulted. She looked hurt. "Didn't you send me an invitation?" she asked.

"Of course I did," I told her. "I posted it with the other invitations. I posted them all at the same time. I bet yours just got lost in the post. Wait a couple more days. Anyway, you know you're invited to the party whether you get your invitation or not."

"But I *want* an invitation!" Nancy demanded.

"I'm sure it'll be waiting for you when you get home from school today," I told her.

It wasn't.

It wasn't there on Thursday afternoon, either.

When Nancy's mother drove Nancy and me to school on Friday morning, Nancy scowled the whole way. Then she waited until we were in our classroom. She waited until Hannie and some other girls were around us and she said, "I suppose Karen didn't invite me after all. I suppose she never posted me an invitation. She doesn't want me at her sleepover. And I've even got my own sleeping bag. I wouldn't need to borrow one."

"I *do* want you at my party!"

I almost shouted that out, but then I remembered about indoor and outdoor voices. So I didn't say it too loudly.

"You don't mean that," said Nancy. She

23

looked embarrassed. Then she looked sad. "I'm the only girl in the class that you haven't invited. And I thought I was one of your best friends."

"You *are*," I told her, just as Miss Colman said, "Time to take your seats, class."

I couldn't talk to Nancy any more. She and Hannie sit in the back row. I sit in the front row with Ricky Torres and Natalie Springer. This is because we wear glasses. No one else in our class does.

And now I know why Nancy doesn't need them. She must have eyes like an eagle. Otherwise, from right at the back of the room, how could she have seen me doodling in my maths book later on? But she did.

She put her hand up.

"Yes, Nancy?" said Miss Colman.

"Karen's drawing in her book," Nancy announced.

Miss Colman looked down at my book where I had drawn:

"Have you finished your work, Karen?" Miss Colman asked me.

I shook my head. "No," I said in a tiny voice. I wanted to turn round and give Nancy a mean look, but I couldn't. Miss Colman was standing right next to me.

"Are you having trouble with the work?" asked Miss Colman.

"No."

"You know you're not supposed to draw in books, don't you?"

"Yes," I replied. My voice was getting smaller and smaller.

"Then you'll have to stay inside during your break today," said Miss Colman. Stay inside! Miss Colman had never punished me before.

"You will have to rub out your drawings

25

and then think about what you did," she told me.

"Okay," I said.

"And Nancy," Miss Colman went on. "No more tale telling, please."

"Okay," said Nancy. "I'm sorry." But she didn't look sorry. Especially when she got to go to break after lunch and I had to go back to our classroom. She looked quite happy about that.

Nancy was *really* angry with me.

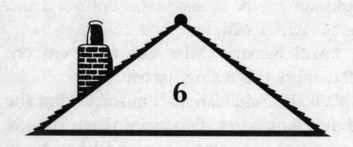

"You're Un-invited!"

Nancy and I didn't speak to each other during the rest of school that day. When she looked at me, I turned my head away. When I looked at her, she did the same thing.

I was very upset. Hardly anyone ever had to miss break. And I was sure Miss Colman was angry with me, even though she didn't act angry.

The thing was, I knew I shouldn't have been drawing in my book. You're not supposed to do that. Unless it is a colouring book, or maybe a workbook. But not a real book. So I *had* done something wrong.

But Nancy had told on me. If I'd seen *her* drawing in *her* book, I wouldn't have told on her. I might have whispered, "Stop that, Nancy," (if I were sitting near her). I might have said, "It isn't nice to draw in books." But I wouldn't have told on her.

Nancy and I didn't have to go home from school together that day. It was a good thing. I was angry with Nancy — and she was *still* angry with me because she hadn't got her invitation.

After school that day, I felt terrible. I couldn't even look forward to going to Daddy's. Andrew and I weren't going there until the next weekend. But guess what would happen then? The sleepover! Next Saturday night would be my sleepover. But thinking about the sleepover didn't make me feel much better.

When our phone rang, I said, "I'll get it!" Maybe it would be Kristy. Talking to Kristy might make me feel better.

I picked up the phone. "Hello?" I said.

"Hi!" cried a voice.

The voice sounded like Nancy's, but it couldn't be.

"Who is this, please?" I asked politely.

"It's *me*, stupid. It's Nancy."

Why was Nancy ringing me?

"Yeah?" I said.

"Guess what?!" Nancy sounded really excited.

"What?"

"It came! It came! The invitation to your sleepover came this afternoon!"

"Good."

"Karen, I — I'm sorry I got you into trouble today. Honestly. I was just angry about the invitation. I promise I'll never tell on you again."

I didn't say anything.

"Okay?" Nancy went on. "I'm *really sorry*. But thank you, thank you, thank you for

inviting me. So — what can I bring to the party?"

"Nothing," I replied. "You're not invited after all. I un-invite you. People who get me into trouble with Miss Colman do *not* come to my sleepovers." I hung up the phone.

Then I ran up to my room. Part of me felt pleased. Now I'd made Nancy feel as bad as she'd made me feel. The other part of me felt awful. I didn't like feeling bad, so Nancy

31

couldn't like feeling bad, either. And I'd made her feel bad.

I didn't know what to think. My thoughts were spinning round and round. Nancy was my best friend. How angry with each other could best friends get? What if we never, ever spoke to each other again?

I almost phoned Nancy back. I almost said, "I'm sorry I un-invited you. Now you're re-invited. You can come after all."

But I just couldn't do that. Nancy had got me into trouble at school. And a best friend isn't supposed to do that.

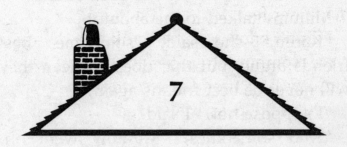

Best Enemies

All that weekend, Nancy and I stayed angry with each other. On Saturday, I invited Hannie over to play. On Sunday, Nancy invited Hannie over to play. But the three of us didn't play together.

On Monday, school started again. Nancy was supposed to travel to Stoneybrook Academy with me, but I didn't want her to. Anyway, she told her mother she would never come in the same car with me again. Not in her whole life.

On Tuesday the same thing happened.

We didn't say a word to each other.

Mummy talked to me about it.

"Karen," she said, "sometimes best friends argue, but that doesn't mean they will never be best friends again."

"I suppose not," I said.

"And sometimes," Mummy went on, "when best friends argue, they hurt each other's feelings. You and Nancy don't want to do that, do you?"

"We already have," I told her. "Anyway, Nancy and I aren't best friends. We're best enemies."

Mummy didn't look happy to hear that.

At school, my sleepover was practically the only thing the girls talked about. Except for Nancy, because she was un-invited.

"I can't wait until Saturday!" exclaimed Jannie Gilbert at break time.

"Me, neither," said Natalie. "I'm going to borrow my sister's sleeping bag. I don't have one of my own."

"I have one," said Leslie Morris.

34

"Me, too," said Hannie and Natalie and several other girls.

"I don't have one," said Jannie. She looked upset.

"Don't worry," I told her. "We have spares."

"Karen, are your brothers going to be at the party?" asked Natalie.

"They might be at home, but they are *not* coming to the party," I replied.

"What if they play tricks on us?" asked Jannie. "What if they give us pepper chewing gum or leave a rubber snake in someone's sleeping bag?"

"Aughh!" shrieked Leslie. "A rubber snake!"

"They won't play tricks," I said. "I won't let them."

"*I* might play tricks," said Ricky. He'd been kicking a football around with some other kids in our grade. Now he was standing with us girls. "You!" I cried. "You're not coming to my party. It's just for girls."

"Yes I am coming," teased Ricky. "And I'm going to throw stones at your window and scare you."

"No!" shrieked Hannie.

"And I'll bring a handful of rubber snakes."

"No!" shrieked Leslie.

"And then I'll spy on you and see all you girls in. . . your underwear!"

I began to laugh. "You aren't going to do those things, Ricky," I said. "And you know it."

Everyone else began to laugh, too.

Everyone except Nancy. She was just standing nearby. She was watching and listening. But she wasn't smiling or laughing. I knew she wanted to come to the party. I felt pretty sorry for her. It isn't fun to be left out of anything. It makes you feel really bad.

But how could I ask my best enemy to come to my sleepover?

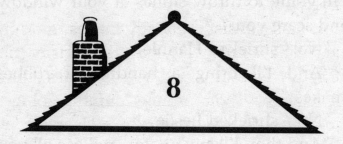

8

The New Girl

You never know about surprises. I suppose that's why they are surprises.

We had a big surprise in Miss Colman's class on Wednesday morning. The school bell had just rung. Hannie and I and everyone else ran for our seats. (Nancy and I still weren't speaking.) I settled down. Ricky settled down next to me.

We smiled at each other.

That was a nice change. We used to throw spitballs instead. Then one of us would tell on the other. That was before we were friends.

Usually, Miss Colman makes morning announcements or takes the register first thing. That morning she said, "Class, I have a surprise. Today, a new pupil is going to join our class. I hope you will make her feel—"

And just then, the door to our room opened. In stepped a girl we'd never seen before. She came in by herself. (If *I* were a new pupil somewhere, I would want Mummy or Daddy to come into the classroom with me. At least on the first day.)

Miss Colman stood with the new girl in front of the room. She put her arm round her. "Boys and girls," she said, "this is Pamela Harding. She's going to be in our class. Karen, would you please show Pamela where the lockers are? Mr Fitzwater" (he's the caretaker) "will be bringing in a desk and chair for Pamela in a few minutes. Until then, Pamela, you may sit at my desk. Okay?"

Pamela nodded.

Lucky duck! I thought. No one else had ever sat at Miss Colman's desk. I showed Pamela the lockers. I waited while she took off her jacket and put her lunch box away.

Then Pamela sat at Miss Colman's desk.

Miss Colman said, "Pamela, maybe you could tell the class about yourself."

"My name is Pamela Harding," said Pamela straight away. "My family have just moved to Stoneybrook. My mother writes books and my father is a dentist. I have a sister. She is sixteen. She lets me wear her perfume."

I was impressed. So were all the other girls. I sneaked a look back at Hannie. She raised her eyebrows at me.

A book writer and a dentist! And a sixteen-year-old sister who let Pamela borrow her perfume!

Besides all that, there was the way Pamela was dressed. I thought she looked cool. Kristy would say she looked trendy. She was wearing baggy pink dungarees and a pink-and-white-striped shirt. On her feet were pink high-top trainers *with the tongues rolled down*. But best of all, on her head was a pink hat. It was *not* a stupid knitted one that you wear on snowy days. It was made of felt. Miss Colman let her wear it indoors. It seemed to be part of the outfit.

No one knew what to make of Pamela. Us girls thought she was beautiful. We wanted her to be our friend. But Pamela didn't say much to us. At lunchtime, she sat by herself. So we moved over to her table.

Pamela still didn't say anything.

At last I said, "I am having a sleepover on Saturday, Pamela. All the girls in our class are coming. Can you come, too?"

Pamela shrugged. She was busy eating her sandwich. "Okay," she replied finally. "I suppose so."

"Great!" I said. Then I narrowed my eyes at Nancy. If we'd been speaking to each other, I would have said, "See? *She* didn't need an invitation in the post."

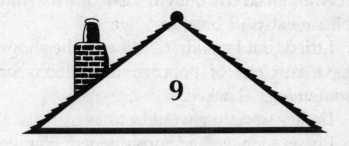

Party Day

Saturday! It had come at last! I was really excited.

In the morning, I leapt out of bed. I didn't even bother to kiss Moosie on the nose. I got dressed as fast as I could. Then I ran downstairs. I ran into the kitchen where Daddy and Elizabeth and Nannie and Emily were having breakfast.

"Okay!" I said. "Let's go shopping! We have to buy all the things on my list. And we can*not* forget balloons. And we have to order the pizzas!"

"Whoa!" said Daddy. "Calm down."

And Elizabeth added, "Sit down. And please eat your breakfast."

I tried, but I couldn't. "What if the shops have run out of popcorn or balloons or something?" I asked.

Daddy said they wouldn't have.

But as soon as the shops opened, Nannie took me shopping. She knew I couldn't wait a minute longer. We drove into town in her old car, which is called the Pink Clinker.

We bought everything we needed. The only thing I felt bad about was Nancy. Should I invite her? No. I just couldn't.

In the afternoon, Kristy helped me get ready for the party. We decided that my guests and I would sleep upstairs in the playroom. That would be fun. Kristy and I blew up balloons. We hung crepe paper and balloons all around the playroom. It looked so, so pretty.

When the room was ready, I decided that I should remind everyone how to behave. I didn't want anyone in my family to do or say something awful in front of Pamela.

"David Michael," I said, "you'd better leave me and my friends alone."

"Don't worry," he replied. "I'm not coming near a bunch of girls."

"Sam, Charlie," I said, "you leave us alone, too."

"Maybe I will and maybe I won't," teased Sam.

Charlie looked serious. "I'll stay out of

your way except for the ghost story," he said.

"Thanks," I replied.

Then I turned to Andrew and Emily. "Andrew, please don't get shy or act like a baby. Emily, please don't dribble food out of your mouth."

Andrew gave me a Cross Look. Emily didn't understand what I'd said.

I could tell that everyone in the big house was glad when the doorbell rang. That meant a guest had arrived. The party would start — and I would stop ordering people around.

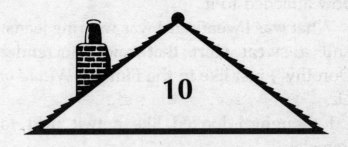

10

Pamela

I flung open our front door. I was all ready to say, "Hi, Hannie!" Since Hannie lives across the street, I was sure she'd be my first guest.

But guess who was standing on our front porch?

Pamela Harding.

And she was dressed up in one of her cool outfits again. She was wearing black trousers with pink pockets on the knees and pink turn-ups at the ankles. And over her trousers she was wearing a *dress* with a flared skirt. In her hair was a headband with a frilly bow attached to it.

What was I wearing? I was wearing jeans, and a sweat shirt that said "Surrender Dorothy", just like in the film *The Wizard of Oz*.

I thought I looked like a twit next to Pamela.

Sam must have thought so, too. He leaned over and whispered in my ear. He called me a dweeb.

I just hoped that the rest of my friends would be wearing jeans, too. Were you *supposed* to get dressed up for a sleepover? Kristy hadn't said so.

"Hi, Pamela," I said. "Come in. You look really nice."

"Thank you," she replied.

She was carrying an overnight bag, but no sleeping bag.

"Oh," I said. "You didn't bring a sleeping bag. Well, that's all right. You can borrow one of ours."

"I won't need one," Pamela replied. "I

have *never* slept on the floor. I *have* to sleep in a bed."

I looked at Elizabeth, who had just come into the front hall. Elizabeth said, "I suppose you can sleep in Karen's bed tonight."

Pamela looked relieved, but I felt worried. What if *all* my friends wanted to sleep in beds?

Luckily they didn't. Soon Hannie, Natalie, Jannie, Leslie and everyone else had arrived. Most of them had brought sleeping bags. The rest wanted to borrow ours. *Nobody* else was dressed up. I felt better.

"Okay!" I said to my friends. "Let's go upstairs to the playroom. That's where we're all going to sleep tonight. So bring your things with you."

"To the *play*room?" repeated Pamela. "You have a playroom?"

I wished Nancy were with me then. She usually knows what to say. She would have said something funny to Pamela.

But *I* just said, "Yes, we have a playroom. I have a little brother and sister."

We all put our sleeping bags on the floor in the playroom. Then we arranged them in a circle, like the spokes of a wagon wheel.

Then we sat on our sleeping bags. (Pamela sat on a chair.) We opened our overnight bags.

"Look what I brought!" cried Leslie. She held up her nightdress. It had leopard spots and a red fringe on it. "It's really for dressing up," she said.

We started to laugh.

"I brought — ta-dah! — my musical puppy," said Jannie. "Look. You push this button on his tummy and he moves his head. *And*, his eyes blink on and off, and a music box inside him plays 'How Much Is That Doggie in the Window?'"

Now we couldn't stop laughing. Except for Pamela, who had never started.

Suddenly — *squirt, squirt, squirt!*

Ugh! We were getting sprayed. We were all wet!

David Michael was standing in the doorway, aiming his water pistol at us.

"Gotcha!" he shouted. Then he ran away.

"Aughh!" we shrieked.

My sleepover had started. But was it off to a good start or a bad start? I wasn't sure.

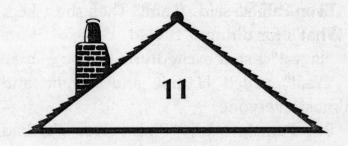

Spook Night

Elizabeth took David Michael's water pistol away from him. She told him not to bother us any more. I thanked her. But I secretly thought that some of my friends had liked his surprise attack.

Oh, well.

It was pizza time.

"Who's hungry?" I asked when everyone had finished drying off. (Pamela was making a big show of patting herself with a towel. I felt bad that David Michael had ruined her hair.)

"I am!" cried my friends.

Even Pamela said, "I am!" Then she asked, "What's for dinner?"

"Pizza!" I said excitedly.

"Yea!" yelled Hannie and Natalie and almost everyone.

But Pamela said, "Pizza gives me bad breath. I can't eat it."

"Oh. Maybe. . . maybe Elizabeth or Kristy can make you something else," I replied.

So Hannie, Leslie, Natalie, and I went to the kitchen. We put paper plates and cups and serviettes and two bottles of lemonade on a tray. Then we picked up the pizza boxes very, very carefully.

As we were leaving the kitchen, Leslie whispered to me, "Karen? Do you think Pamela is having fun?"

Before I could answer, Hannie said, "I think Pamela is. . . well, I don't think *she* is any fun. She makes me feel like a baby."

I didn't know what to say. I felt the same way, but I didn't want to admit it. Anyway, we had to stop talking about Pamela because we'd almost reached the playroom again.

"Here we are!" I said.

Everyone was sitting on their sleeping bags again. (Well, except Pamela.) They made a mad grab for the pizzas and lemonade and began to eat on their laps.

"My big sister is making you a sandwich," I told Pamela. "Peanut butter and jam. But only a little peanut butter, in case you're afraid it will stick to the roof of your mouth, or give you peanut-butter breath."

Hannie giggled. The other girls looked at Pamela warily. I think most of them still wanted her to like them. I bet Nancy wouldn't care, though, if she were here. And I wished she were. She wouldn't stand for what Pamela was doing.

"Okay, time for a spooky film," I said. (We have a video *and* a TV in our playroom.) "Guess what I've chosen to watch with our dinner?"

"What?" asked Leslie.

"The Wizard of Oz!"

"Ooh, goody!" exclaimed Jannie. "The witch is so scary."

"So are the flying monkeys," said someone else.

From her chair, Pamela sighed. "That's a film for babies," she said.

"Is not!" said the rest of us.

I decided that Pamela didn't count. We watched the film and ate our pizza while Pamela combed her hair and ate the sandwich Kristy had brought her.

My friends and I got scareder and scareder.

When Dorothy was trapped in the witch's castle and the face of the Wicked Witch of the West appeared in the crystal ball, Hannie even screamed.

And then. . . from outside. . . BLAM! A huge clap of thunder sounded.

All the rest of us began to scream, too. A storm was coming. A big one.

I could tell we were going to have a spook night.

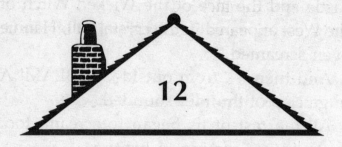

The Ricky Torres
Dough Boy

During the rest of the film, my friends just sat and stared. The pizza was eaten. The storm was coming. We were glued to the TV. We couldn't think of anything except the witch and her broomstick and her castle.

We were so, so scared.

Finally Dorothy woke up from her dream. She was saying, "There's no place like home. There's no place like home." That was when we all let out sighs of relief.

"Whew!" said Leslie. "I didn't think she was going to make it."

"Haven't you ever seen the film before?" asked Pamela.

"No," replied Leslie. "Have you?"

"Only about eighty-seven times. We own the film.

"Well, so do we, but it still scares me," I said. I felt like sticking up for Leslie.

Boy, did I wish Nancy was at my party. If you think I have a big mouth, you should hear Nancy. She says whatever she wants. She told me once that this is because she plans to be an actress one day. She says it is good practice.

I turned off the video. "Who wants to make cookies?" I asked.

"What kind?" Hannie wanted to know.

"Slice 'n' Bake with chocolate chips."

"Oh, yum! They're the best kind!" cried Leslie. "You can slice them up — which is really easy. Or you can make them into shapes!"

We carried the empty pizza boxes and all

59

our rubbish downstairs. We threw everything away. Then I called, "Kristy! Can you come and help us bake cookies?"

"Okay!" she called back.

(I'm not allowed to touch the cooker or the oven. A grown-up has to do that for me.)

"How come your sister is babysitting for you?" Pamela asked me.

"She is *not* babysitting. She's just helping," I told her.

Then I decided to ignore Pamela. I joined Hannie and Natalie, who were slicing cookies, but eating about every other slice.

There is just nothing like raw cookie dough.

Before we had even put a tray of slices in the oven, Leslie rolled some dough into a ball and threw it at Jannie. Jannie giggled and threw it back. Soon we were having a dough ball fight. Even Kristy joined in. We were giggling and shrieking and running around. (Pamela sat at the kitchen table. Her chin rested in her hand. She looked bored out of her mind. She didn't even move when a piece of dough hit her head.)

The next thing I knew, the fight was over. And Natalie was holding up something she had made. "Who does this look like?" she asked.

"Ricky Torres!" I said.

It *was* Ricky. We baked him with the other cookies. When the timer went off, we watched Kristy take the cookies out of the oven.

"Who wants to eat Ricky?" she asked.

At first, no one could bear to eat the Ricky Torres Dough Boy. Finally Hannie said, "I'll eat him." She bit his head off.

"Aughh!" cried Kristy from behind her. "That hurt!"

Everyone laughed. Pamela looked bored. So I began to feel bad.

Kristy pulled me aside. "Are you having fun?" she asked me.

I shook my head. "No. Pamela Harding is ruining everything. . . . I wish Nancy was here."

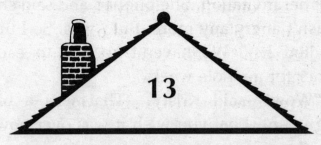

"Please Come to My Sleepover!"

"Karen?" said Kristy. She had taken me into the study. My party guests were in the kitchen. They were eating the Slice 'n' Bake cookies and drinking milk.

"Yes?" I answered.

"Where *is* Nancy? Is she ill or something?"

I sighed. "No. We had an argument."

"About what?"

"Nancy didn't get her invitation in the post when everyone else did. She thought I hadn't invited her to my party. So she was annoyed and she told on me and got me into trouble with Miss Colman. *Then* Nancy got her invitation. She phoned and said she wasn't angry any more. But *I* was. So I uninvited her. We haven't spoken to each other for a whole week."

"Wow!" said Kristy. "That was a big argument. I bet you wish it was over now, don't you?"

"Do I ever! I really need Nancy here. She'd know what to do about Pamela. But what I really want is to make it up with Nancy. I don't know how to do that, though. And I feel funny inviting her to my party *now*."

"I think you should phone her," said Kristy. "Apologize to her. She's already apologized to you. And say you forgive her for getting you into trouble. She was just angry then, Karen. People do all sorts of things when they're angry. And I bet Nancy would rather come to your party late than not at all."

I thought about that. "I don't know. Maybe. . . ."

"*Phone* her," said Kristy. "It's the mature thing to do."

Well. I *am* a very mature person for a seven-year-old. So I said, "Okay. I'll phone her."

Kristy left the study so that I could have some privacy. She said she would help my friends make more cookies.

My heart pounded as I dialled the number. Mrs Dawes answered.

"Hi," I said in a small voice. "This is Karen. Is Nancy there?"

"Yes, she is. Hold on a sec."

As soon as Nancy got on the phone I started talking. I wanted to get things over with quickly. Like ripping a plaster off fast instead of peeling it back slowly.

"Nancy, I'm really sorry I un-invited you to my party," I said. "But you made me feel bad when you got me into trouble. I know you feel bad now, though. So I think our row should be over. And I want you to come to my party straight away."

"You do? Thanks! And Karen, I *am* sorry

I got you into trouble. That was a horrible thing to do. Do you forgive me?"

"Oh, yes!" I said, remembering what Kristy had told me. "I forgive you. Do *you* forgive *me*?"

"Yes, I do."

"Good. Then come over right now. You won't believe Pamela. She's making us all feel like babies."

"She is? How?"

"She thought *The Wizard of Oz* wasn't a scary film, when everyone knows it is. I mean, duh. And she won't sleep in a sleeping bag. And she wouldn't eat pizza with us. She said it gives her bad breath. Now she's just sitting there while everyone else makes cookies. She looks like she thinks we are idiots. Maybe even dweebs. She's ruining everything. Please come to my sleepover. I really need you!"

So of course Nancy got permission from her parents. Her father said he would drive her over straight away.

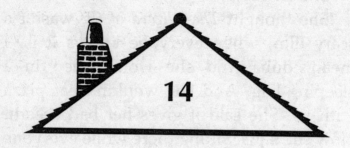

14

Blackout

Flash! Flash! BLAM! BLAM!

Lightning lit up our garden. Thunder thundered. The storm was on its way — but there was no rain yet.

The rain didn't start until Nancy arrived. She ran to our door and rang the bell three times fast. Just as she had climbed out of her daddy's car, the rain had begun to fall in huge, gusty sheets.

When I opened the door, though, Nancy was only a little bit wet. But she wanted to get inside fast.

" 'Bye!" she called to her father.

Mr Dawes waved. Then he drove away.

I closed the door behind Nancy. We hugged tightly. Hannie smiled at us. She was glad our argument was over.

"Here," I said to Nancy. "Let me take your things. Hey, how come you've brought two sleeping bags?" Nancy was wearing a rucksack and had been carrying a sleeping bag in each hand.

(Flash! BLAM!)

"Yeah," said Jannie. "How come?" Everybody had rushed into the front hall to greet Nancy.

"I heard that Pamela doesn't have a sleeping bag, so I brought one along for her."

I tried not to giggle. So did Hannie and Natalie.

"I *sleep* in *beds*," was all Pamela would say.

"How boring," replied Nancy. Without waiting for Pamela to reply, she went on, "Boy, what a storm! It is so, so scary out there. My father said we're really in for it."

"What's that supposed to mean?" asked Pamela.

"It means we're in great danger," said Nancy in a low voice.

Even Pamela looked scared at that.

Then I said, "Maybe this is a good time for Charlie to tell us a ghost story. He promised he would."

"Ooh," said Leslie. "I don't know. . . ."

"Oh, it will only be fun scary," I told her. "Honest."

So I found Charlie, and we sat on the sleeping bags in the playroom again. Pamela started out on a chair. But as Charlie told the story, she began edging off it.

Charlie's story was about a ghost that haunts a huge mansion. The people in the house only see him when it rains. The ghost wears a bucket on his head, so the family calls him Buckethead. This makes the ghost angry.

"I will get you! I will get revenge!" wails the ghost.

Pamela slid all the way off her chair. Now

she was sitting on the floor.

I looked at Nancy. She was looking at me. Her eyes were shining. Very quietly, she reached over and turned off a lamp.

"Aughh!" shrieked everyone except Charlie and Nancy and me.

Pamela moved onto Jannie's sleeping bag.

"The people in the house," Charlie was saying, "heard clanking sounds. . . like chains being rattled. A girl saw a white figure standing at the end of her bed one night. The figure said, 'I will taaaake my reveeeenge soooooon.'"

"Ooh," whispered Hannie.

Outside, the wind howled. The rain beat on the windows. Just as Buckethead was taking his revenge, a bolt of lightning lit up the playroom.

Then the lights went out.

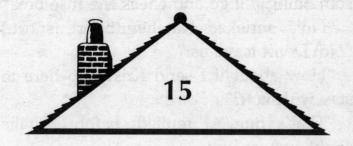

"Where Am I?"

"Help! Oh, help!" Was that Pamela's voice? I couldn't be sure.

"Where am I? I can't see a thing!" cried someone else.

It was true. I held my hand out in front of my face. I couldn't see it.

All around me, my friends were screaming. Some of them were even crying. I knew for certain that Natalie was crying, because she snorts when she cries.

"Calm down, everyone!" I heard Charlie

say. "We've probably just blown a fuse or something. I'll go and check the fuse box."

"No!" shrieked Natalie. (Snort, snort.) "No! Don't leave us!"

"How about if I send Kristy up here to stay with you?"

"That's fine," I replied, before Natalie could answer him.

In a few minutes I could see a light bobbing down the hallway.

"Eeeee! It's Buckethead!" cried Natalie. (Snort, snort.)

"Who's Buckethead?" That was Kristy. She was making the bobbing light. She was running through the hallway with a torch.

"It's only my sister," I announced to my party guests. "Don't worry."

Kristy was carrying three more torches with her. She put them on the floor and turned them on. The room looked spooky and shadowy, but at least we could see again.

Natalie was still crying. Actually, she was the only one crying. My other friends looked

scared but okay. Pamela found her chair
again.

"I'm frightened," wailed Natalie.

"Wimp," muttered Pamela.

"Did Charlie look at the fuse box?" I asked
Kristy.

"He didn't need to," she replied. "And
I'm afraid I have a little bit of bad news."

"Oh, no!" cried Natalie. (Snort.)

"What kind of bad news?" I asked.

"It's not a problem with our fuse box. There's a blackout. We looked outside. There are no lights on anywhere. That means nobody in our neighbourhood has any power."

Natalie snorted and said she wanted to go home.

Pamela called her a wimp again.

Then Leslie said, "My big brother told me that thunder is really dead people bowling, and if a bowling ball rolls into the gutter, it will fall out of the sky. It could crash straight through the roof of your house."

"*My* brother," began Jannie, "says that lightning is caused by angry ghosts. And if they're angry enough, they'll send a lightning bolt right down to the ground."

Hannie began to cry then, too (at least she doesn't snort), so Kristy said, "Haven't any of you heard about cold fronts and warm fronts?"

In the dim light I saw Pamela yawn.

"Cold fronts and warm fronts?" Nancy repeated.

"Yes," said Kristy. "A thunderstorm is *just weather*. That's *all*. When air is unstable — when it rises up instead of staying still — and if the air is wet, too, then you get a thunderstorm. You see, the big, dark thunderclouds are charged with electricity. . . ."

"Do you know what she's talking about?" I heard Leslie whisper to Natalie.

"No." Natalie didn't even snort.

And just at that moment, the power returned. All the lights came on again.

"Hurray!" cheered my friends.

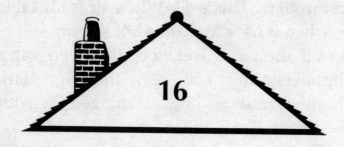

Bedtime

With the lights on again, the playroom looked very cheerful. My friends and I didn't feel scared at all any more.

"Do you all know enough about thunderstorms now?" asked Kristy.

"Yes!" we cried.

"Because I could teach you some more things—"

"NO!" we shouted. We began to giggle. Kristy left then. Jannie turned on her musical puppy. I tried to turn a cartwheel over the sleeping bags (I fell down), and

Nancy threw a stuffed toy at Hannie. Hannie shrieked and threw it back.

"Ahem!"

Uh-oh. That was Daddy. I could tell without even turning around.

Everyone stopped what they were doing.

"Girls?" said Daddy.

"Yes?" I sat up and looked at him.

"Bedtime now, okay? You've had plenty of excitement for one night."

I looked at my watch. It was only ten o'clock. My friends and I had planned to stay up until at least midnight. But all I said was, "All right. 'Night, Daddy. We'll get ready for bed now."

"Sleep tight, girls," said Daddy. Then he left.

My friends began groaning. They said things like, "Karen, do we have to go to bed *now*?" And, "But, Karen, it's too *early*!"

Pamela said, "I go to bed at ten o'clock on *school* nights."

I smiled. "We're not *really* going to bed now. We're just going to pretend. We'll put on our pyjamas and get into our sleeping bags—"

"Or beds," interrupted Pamela.

"Whatever. Anyway," I went on, "then we'll talk and tell stories until midnight. And *then* we're going to do something special. We'll do it in the dark when Daddy and Elizabeth and everyone else in the house is asleep," I said, very mysteriously.

"What is it?" whispered Hannie with wide eyes.

"Secret," I replied. "Now, come on. Let's get ready for bed before Daddy comes back and has to tell us a second time. Sometimes he gets annoyed if he has to tell me things twice."

So my friends and I put on our pyjamas. Everyone agreed that Leslie's leopard-skin nightdress was the best. Pamela went into the bathroom. She washed her face. She brushed her teeth. The rest of us didn't bother. We knew those things didn't matter at a sleepover.

When she had finished, she stood in the doorway to the playroom.

"Are you *sure* you don't want to borrow my extra sleeping bag?" asked Nancy sweetly. "I brought it just for you."

"I'm very sure," said Pamela.

I tried not to laugh. Instead I said, "Come on, Pamela. I'll show you where my room is. I hope you like my bed."

Pamela and I walked down the hall to my room. Pamela was just about to climb into my bed when she stopped. "What are *those*?" she asked, pointing to the end of my bed.

"They are Tickly and Moosie," I told her.

"*Baby* things?" she asked, picking one up with her fingertips.

"No!" I exclaimed. I grabbed Tickly and Moosie and gave them a hug.

"Do you still sleep with them?" asked Pamela.

I didn't answer her. Pamela got into my bed.

"See you at midnight," I told her.

And since she was such a grown-up, I didn't turn on my night-light or leave the door open a crack. I left her in pitch blackness. Then I returned to my friends. *They* wouldn't make fun of my blanket or my stuffed cat.

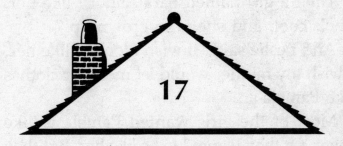

Midnight

I'd been afraid that staying awake until midnight might be hard. Last year, I'd tried to stay awake until midnight on New Year's Eve, but I couldn't do it. I fell asleep. Luckily, Mummy and Seth woke me up just in time to yell, "Hurray! Happy New Year!"

But at my sleepover, nobody had any trouble staying awake. Even with the lights out. The very first thing that happened after we were supposed to be asleep was that Nancy asked a question.

She said, "Who here likes Pamela?"

At first nobody said a word.

Then a girl named Sara said, "*I* like her. She's cool, and she is so grown-up."

And Leslie said, "I wish I looked like her. I wish my mother would let me wear clothes like Pamela's.

Most of the girls wanted Pamela to like them. Or they wanted to be like her. But they didn't say they *liked Pamela*.

Finally Nancy said, "I think Pamela is an idiot."

Jannie gasped.

It was time to change the subject. "What," I began in a low voice, "is the scariest thing that has ever happened to anyone here?"

"Getting lost at Disney World," said Natalie right away.

"That happened to me once, too!" I exclaimed.

We told scary stories and funny stories and embarrassing stories for a long, long time. Finally I turned on one of the torches that Kristy had brought to the playroom. I looked at my watch.

"Hey, everyone! It's almost midnight!" I said in a loud whisper.

"You'd better go and get Pamela," said Sara.

"Oh," I groaned, but I tiptoed to my room anyway. I opened the door. "Hey, Pamela," I said. "It's almost midnight. It's time for the secret surprise."

No answer. I shone the torch in Pamela's face. She was sound asleep. I decided to leave her that way. She probably needed her beauty sleep.

I went back to the playroom and told my friends I couldn't wake up Pamela. Then I said, "Guess what. Now it is time to. . . raid the fridge!"

"Yea!" yelled a couple of girls.

"SHHH!" I hissed. "We have to be very quiet, and we cannot turn on any lights."

I passed round the torches and we tiptoed downstairs. On the way, Jannie crashed into a table. We were all quiet for a few moments, but I didn't hear Daddy or Elizabeth getting up. So we went towards the kitchen.

When we got there, we had to leave the light off.

"We don't want anyone to know we're awake," I reminded my friends.

Then we opened the fridge door. There was leftover apple pie and bread and lots of nice things for making sandwiches. There was also fruit and lemonade and milk.

"Help yourselves!" I said.

But just then I heard a low growl. I looked at the doorway to the kitchen. Floating in the air was a glowing monster head. It didn't have a body.

"Aughh!" I shrieked.

"Aughh!" shrieked my friends.

The monster turned on a light. It was just Sam. He was shining a torch behind a scary mask.

"Sam!" I exclaimed.

"What's going on here?" (Uh-oh. That was Daddy.) "Everybody back to bed," he said. "And I mean it."

So we went to bed for real this time. We didn't even get to raid the fridge.

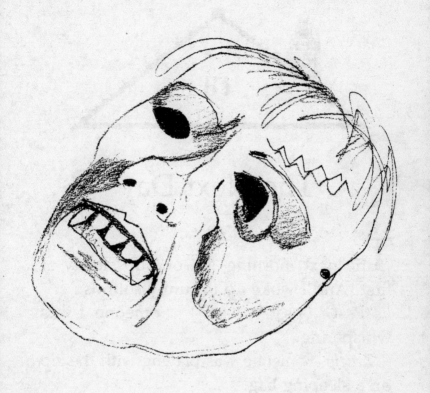

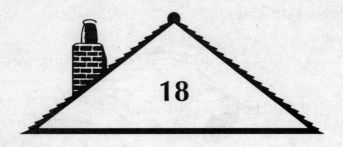

The Next Day

The next morning, I woke up slowly at first. And I woke up to funny sounds.

"Psst, psst, psst." Someone was whispering.

Zzzzip. Someone was playing with the zip on a sleeping bag.

Creeeak. Someone was tiptoeing across the room.

Who *are* all these people? I thought. And why are they in my bedroom? Then I remembered my sleepover. The people were my friends, and I was in the playroom in a sleeping bag on the floor. Suddenly I was wide awake.

"Morning!" I said, sitting up.

"Morning," replied Hannie, cheerfully. "Guess what time it is."

"Seven-thirty?" I asked.

"Nope. Ten o'clock."

"Ten o'clock!" I cried. "We've wasted half the morning! Everybody get up. It's breakfast time. It's almost *lunch*time!"

Soon my friends and I were up and dressed. We cleared up the playroom. We rolled up our sleeping bags. Then I had to go and get Pamela before we went downstairs.

"Where are your blanky and aminal?" she asked in a baby voice.

"Never mind," I replied.

My friends and I went into the kitchen. Daddy and Nannie were there.

"Well, here are the sleepyheads," said Nannie, smiling.

And Daddy said, "How about a picnic breakfast in the garden?"

I looked outside. I remembered the storm the night before. But the sun was shining now and the sky was blue.

"Okay!" I said. "Thanks, Daddy."

The ground was still wet from the rain, so we spread out plastic mats. Then we put blankets over them. Nannie made pancakes and bacon, and then Daddy helped us carry our plates outside. We were starving. We ate two helpings of everything — except for Leslie, who doesn't like pancakes. (She's

the only person I know who doesn't like them.) And Nancy didn't eat any bacon. She never eats pork.

"Why?" asked Jannie.

"Because my family is Jewish," Nancy replied. "And Mummy and Daddy say, 'No pork.' I don't like bacon anyway."

We were just finishing our breakfast when we heard a car horn. Someone had pulled up in front of the big house.

"Karen!" Elizabeth called. "Jannie's mother is here." So Jannie had to leave.

I wished very hard that the next parent to arrive would be one of Pamela's. My wish came true. Mr Harding arrived next. Pamela gathered up her things. It took her a long time, even though she didn't have a sleeping bag. I wasn't sorry to see Pamela go. She had been really mean about Moosie, Tickly, and a lot of other things. I decided I didn't want to be Pamela's friend, no matter what.

I wanted to tell her those things.

But I didn't do it. Not in front of the other girls.

All I said was, " 'Bye, Pamela. Thanks for coming. See you at school!"

I heaved a huge sigh of relief.

Then I turned to smile at Hannie and Nancy.

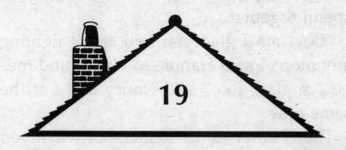

The Three Musketeers

Pretty soon, everyone had gone — everyone except Hannie and Nancy. Hannie lived so near by that she could walk home. We didn't know where Nancy's parents were but we hoped they were at home. We wanted to ask them if Nancy could spend the day at the big house. Hannie already had permission.

Guess what? We called the Dawes' and they were still at home. They said it would be okay for Mummy to take Nancy home when she picked up Andrew and me that afternoon.

So all three of us had a whole day to spend together.

"Boy, am I glad you two aren't fighting any more," said Hannie to Nancy and me.

"I'm glad, too," said Nancy and I at the same time.

Then Nancy said, "Remember when you and Hannie had an argument?"

"Yup," I replied, and added, "Remember when *you* and Hannie had an argument?"

"Yup," said Nancy.

"Boy, we should stop arguing," I said. "We're lucky we're friends. If we weren't friends, we might have to be friends with Pamela."

"Oh, yuck!" said Nancy to Hannie.

"You know what?" I said. "We're like the Three Musketeers."

"Hey!" cried Nancy. "I've got a great idea. We should become blood sisters!"

"Blood sisters?" repeated Hannie.

"Yeah," said Nancy. "We prick our fingers. Then when the blood comes out, we mix it all up so we each have a little of our friends' blood."

"Ugh!" cried Hannie. "That sounds disgusting."

"We could try it anyway," I said.

I wasn't sure that this was a good idea. Even so, I found a needle. I washed it with antiseptic so it would be clean. Then I handed it to Nancy. "You go first," I told her.

"Prick my *own* finger? No way!" she exclaimed.

"Well, don't prick mine," said Hannie. "I really don't think we should mix up our blood. Even if it would make us blood sisters."

"Don't look at me," I said to Nancy. "I don't want you to prick me, either. I do not think it is safe."

"Neither do I," said Nancy finally.

So in the end we decided to be just the Three Musketeers, not blood sisters.

We drew up a pact. It looked like this:

WE ARE THE THREE MUSKETEERS
WE VOW TO BE FRIENDS FOR LIFE.
SIGNED,
Karen Brewer
Nancy Dawes
Hannie Papadakis

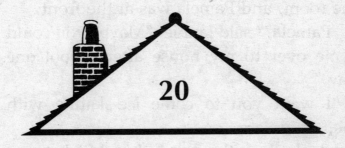

20

School Again

"Look. Look at my new outfit!" said Pamela Harding.

It was Monday. It was the day after Nancy and Hannie and I became the Three Musketeers. We were back at school, and Pamela was prancing around our classroom. She was wearing a bright green dress made from sweat shirt material, black tights, and over the tights, green ankle socks. But best of all, on her feet were high-topped moccasins with a fringe.

I bet you could smell her sister's perfume

a mile away. I could smell it at the back of the room, and Pamela was at the front.

"Pamela?" said Jannie. "Maybe you could come over to my house after school one day."

"I want you to come ice-skating with me," said Sara.

I looked at the two other Musketeers. "Don't Jannie and Sara remember how awful Pamela was at the sleepover?" I asked them.

"I suppose not," answered Nancy, "but I don't care. If those girls want to be friends with Pamela, then let them."

"Yeah," said Hannie. "We've got each other. We're the Three Musketeers now."

"Oh, Hannie! We have your copy of the pact," I said.

The night before, Nancy and I had given the pact to Nancy's daddy. Mr Dawes had made two copies of it on his photocopier at home. One copy was for Nancy and one was for Hannie. I kept the real pact, the one we'd actually signed.

"Thanks," said Nancy, when I gave her the copy.

Then Nancy pulled her copy out of the pocket of her jeans. I pulled the real pact out of my rucksack.

We read the pact aloud together.

"We are the Three Musketeers. We vow to be friends for life."

"Maybe," I said, watching Pamela, "we should add something to our pact. Something like, 'And we vow never to be friends with Pamela Harding.'"

"I like our pact the way it is," said Hannie. She was reading hers again.

"Who cares about Pamela, anyway?" asked Nancy.

"*They* do," I replied. I pointed to the girls who had surrounded Pamela. Pamela was showing off every inch of her outfit.

I wondered if the girls were more impressed with Pamela or her clothes. And then something occurred to me. The girls in the class liked Pamela's glamour. But they didn't know the real Pamela underneath.

Would they find out? If they did find out and they didn't like her, would they care?

Well, I knew one thing. Even if Pamela became Queen of the Classroom, the Three Musketeers would stick together. I said so to Hannie and Nancy.

"Right," said Hannie.

"Through thick and thin," said Nancy.

"Forever and ever," I added.

We invented a secret Three Musketeers handshake. We clapped our hands once, we made a tower out of our fists, then we snapped our fingers twice. It was really cool.

"Hi!" said Natalie Springer just then. She joined my friends and me at the back of the room. She had left the crowd round Pamela. "You know what?" she said to me. "Your sleepover was the best ever. Even though I've never been to one before."

Ricky came over to us, too. "Hey," he said. "I heard your sleepover was really good fun. Can I come to the next one?"

"Maybe," I said, smiling.

And when Natalie and Ricky were gone, us Three Musketeers did our secret handshake again.

BABYSITTERS LITTLE SISTER

Meet Karen Brewer aged 6. Already known to Babysitters fans as Kristy's little sister, for the very first time she features in a series of her very own.

THE BABYSITTERS CLUB

Need a babysitter? Then call the Babysitters Club. Kristy Thomas and her friends are all experienced sitters. They can tackle any job from rampaging toddlers to a pandemonium of pets. To find out all about them, read on!

MYSTERY THRILLERS

Introducing a new series of hard-hitting action-packed thrillers for young adults.

THE SONG OF THE DEAD by Anthony Masters
For the first time in years "the song of the dead" is heard around Whitstable. Is it really the cries of dead sailors? Or is it something more sinister? Barney Hampton is determined to get to the bottom of the mystery . . .

THE FERRYMAN'S SON by Ian Strachan
Rob is convinced that Drewe and Miles are up to no good. Where do they go on their night cruises? And why does Kimberley go with them? When Kimberley disappears Rob finds himself embroiled in a web of deadly intrigue . . .

TREASURE OF GREY MANOR by Terry Deary
When Jamie Williams and Trish Grey join forces for a school history project, they unearth much more than they bargain for! The diary of the long-dead Marie Grey hints at the existence of hidden treasure. But Jamie and Trish aren't the only ones interested in the treasure – and some people don't mind playing dirty . . .

THE FOGGIEST by Dave Belbin
As Rachel and Matt Gunn move into their new home, a strange fog descends over the country. Then Rachel and Matt's father disappears from his job at the weather station, and they discover the sinister truth behind the fog . . .

BLUE MURDER by Jay Kelso
One foggy night Mack McBride is walking along the pier when he hears a scream and a splash. Convinced that a murder has been committed he decides to investigate and finds himself in more trouble than he ever dreamed of . . .